Benny Dubious Playbook Scheme: Nevada Shuffle
By
Maxwell Hoffman

Benny Dubious Playbook Scheme: Nevada Shuffle

Benny Dubiuos Playbook Scheme Nevada Shuffle, Volume 1

Maxwell Hoffman

Published by Maxwell Hoffman, 2024.

This is a work of fiction. Similarities to real people, places, or events are entirely coincidental.

BENNY DUBIOUS PLAYBOOK SCHEME: NEVADA SHUFFLE

First edition. November 9, 2024.

Copyright © 2024 Maxwell Hoffman.

ISBN: 979-8227917065

Written by Maxwell Hoffman.

Benny Dubious Playbook Scheme: Nevada Shuffle

Benny Dubiuos Playbook Scheme Nevada Shuffle, Volume 1

Maxwell Hoffman

Published by Maxwell Hoffman, 2024.

This is a work of fiction. Similarities to real people, places, or events are entirely coincidental.

BENNY DUBIOUS PLAYBOOK SCHEME: NEVADA SHUFFLE

First edition. November 9, 2024.

Copyright © 2024 Maxwell Hoffman.

ISBN: 979-8227917065

Written by Maxwell Hoffman.

Also by Maxwell Hoffman

Acorn Man Savior of the Forest
Acorn Man Savior of the Forest

Arctic Shadows: A Lenin Aslanov Story
Arctic Shadows: A Lenin Aslanov Story Book 1: The Finnish Incursion

Baron Floofnose: A Capybara's Quest
Baron Floofnose: A Capybara's Quest Omnibus Trilogy

Benny Dubious Playbook Scheme Series 3
Benny Dubious Playbook Scheme Trouble in Georgia Book 2: "Moshie's" Fall
Benny Dubious Playbook Scheme Trouble in Georgia Book 3: Hugo's Revelation

Benny Dubiuos Playbook Scheme Nevada Shuffle
Benny Dubious Playbook Scheme: Nevada Shuffle

Frozen Dawn: A Neanderthal's Redemption
Frozen Dawn: A Neanderthal's Redemption Omnibus Trilogy

Ivan Zhuk: Zhuk's Gambit
Ivan Zhuk: Zhuk's Gambit Book 1 Mental Agony
Ivan Zhuk: Zhuk's Gambit Book 2 The MMA Fighter
Ivan Zhuk: Zhuk's Gambit Book 3 Ivan's Freedom

Knox Sovereign: The Juche Wars
Knox Sovereign: The Juche Wars Book 1 Unmasking Knox Sovereign
Knox Sovereign: The Juche Wars Book 2 A Daring Rescue
Knox Sovereign: The Juche Wars Book 3: Fall of Colonel Rex MacManners

Misadventures of Wolfgang Wirrarr
Misadventures of Wolfgang Wirrarr Omnibus Trilogy

Rowan Sunfire Frosty Fugitive Series
Rowan Sunfire Frosty Fugitive Book 3 Defense of Vos Tower
Rowan Sunfire Frosty Fugitive Omnibus Trilogy

Wiccan Guardian
Wiccan Guardian Omnibus Trilogy

Watch for more at https://www.instagram.com/vader7800/.

Table of Contents

Title Page 1

Episode 1: Taxes are Due and a Job from Zafar! 11

Episode 2: The Nevada Trucking Trucker Company Building 15

Episode 3: Suspicious Manager Bao Luc 19

Episode 4: Benny Runs for It! 23

Episode 5: Red, White and Secure Asset 27

Episode 6: Resting Benny and Kassim Plots 31

Episode 7: Getting Mina Involved 35

Episode 8: Disorganized Benny 39

Episode 9: Blackmailing Zafar 43

Episode 10: Kassim's Place 47

Episode 11: Encounter with Kassim! 51

Episode 12: Unhappy Kassim 55

Episode 13: Epilogue 59

Table of Contents

Title Page 1

Episode 1: Taxes are Due and a Job from Zafar! 11

Episode 2: The Nevada Trucking Trucker Company Building 15

Episode 3: Suspicious Manager Bao Luc 19

Episode 4: Benny Runs for It! 23

Episode 5: Red, White and Secure Asset 27

Episode 6: Resting Benny and Kassim Plots 31

Episode 7: Getting Mina Involved 35

Episode 8: Disorganized Benny 39

Episode 9: Blackmailing Zafar 43

Episode 10: Kassim's Place 47

Episode 11: Encounter with Kassim! 51

Episode 12: Unhappy Kassim 55

Episode 13: Epilogue 59

Episode 1: Taxes are Due and a Job from Zafar!

It's Benny's first year in Las Vegas since he managed to escape from Los Angeles. Already thanks to the money that Khalid Jared Muhammad had given to him, Benny could start up his own casino. Much of this wouldn't be possible without the help of Benny's close friend Zafar Mehmet who was already in Las Vegas.

"My new place to call home" said Benny as he gazed around the casino.

It was a rather empty place. There was hardly a customer lining up let alone workers to be hired.

"Wow, I need to start advertising about my casino" continued Benny.

But as the mail carrier came by, the carrier soon delivered the mail. Benny gasped at one of the letters - it was from the Department of Taxation! Benny couldn't believe that Nevada's version of the California Franchise Tax Board was issuing demands that he pay up.

"The nerve that they're letting me know that I didn't pay them!" said Benny.

Benny decided to alert his friend Zafar Mehmet on what to do next. Zafar unlike Benny, was always studious on filing his taxes. This even with him being involved with the shady White Batch back in Los Angeles.

"Yes Benny?" asked Zafar as he picked up the phone.

"I need help, the Neveda Department of Taxation sent me a letter" said Benny.

"Did you remember to file your taxes on time?" asked Zafar. Benny shook his head.

"Sadly no, I was too busy setting everything up and filing paperwork" continued Benny.

"Send me a photo copy of the letter to see how much you owe" continued Zafar.

Benny sighed. It was a hefty fine - worth at least 100K! Benny took a photo with his cellphone and sent it to Zafar.

"Tsk, tsk, tsk, Benny did you not tell them other sources of income?" asked Zafar.

"Well, I was too busy setting up my casino" continued Benny.

"Excuses, excuses" sighed Zafar.

Zafar was perplexed to how Benny Dubious rose through the ranks on becoming Khalid Jared Muhammad's right-hand man of the White Batch. Even leading recruitment efforts in Los Angeles by meeting with various White Batch members. All of this could soon be investigated as possible illegal activities by the authorities.

"You already fled one state because of your deeds, you shouldn't flee this one" continued Zafar.

Zafar knew his money was already tied up in certain transactions, however he felt confident Benny could do this one job for him.

"Benny, I will be more than happy to pay for your fine, but you have to do a job for me first" said Zafar.

"Anything, you name it" continued Benny.

Zafar thought of an easy task for Benny. He was going to go down to a trucking company that owed Zafar money.

"I need you to drive down to a trucking company, they have failed to pay the monthly fee to ensure my shipments will get through" continued Zafar.

Benny was excited that he finally got to do something while in Las Vegas. He headed towards the drawer in his office and got out a handgun.

"The trucking company isn't far from where your casino is" said Zafar.

Benny was pleased to follow orders from Zafar. He headed out towards his car and started to drive off. Benny took note of the name of the trucking company - Nevada Truckers. They were one of many trucking companies that would often ship around goods from Zafar's shipping company.

"Ah, here we are" said Benny as he parked the car.

Benny soon realized this place had some heavy security. He could tell by the number of guards surrounding the place. Why would so many guards be necessary for a mere trucking company? Unless Benny thought they were doing more illegal activities than him! Benny would need to be careful in approaching this.

Episode 2: The Nevada Trucking Trucker Company Building

Benny dove around the corner and noticed there were so many security guards. For a trucking company, they certainly have so much security. He would have to sneak pass them and gain access.

"Great, I have to get past them but how?" thought Benny.

Benny could see the security guards' routine as he continued to sneak by. He could see a number of them were heavily armed which was strange for a trucking company. Now why would a trucking company need armed security? Unless they were doing some illegal activities! Benny continued to dodge the security guards as they continued on their patrols.

"Nothing out of the ordinary" said one security guard.

"Nope, boss wants to keep everything secured" added a second security guard, "it's a good thing that this Zafar Mehmet doesn't realize his main competitor was behind getting the Nevada Truckers to stop doing business with his shipping company."

Benny remained cautious as he continued to trek around the back area of the building. Why would Zafar's competitor be invested in a trucking company? Benny needed to find out more answers, he made his way towards the back area of the building. Not much security as there were in the front.

"Ha, such fools" laughed Benny.

Benny then noticed a back door, as he tried to open it, it was locked. He wondered if one of the security guards had the key to the back door. He would need to hid in a nearby alleyway and observe the movements. As Benny ducked around some trash cans in the alleyway, he stayed in his position watching and waiting. He then noticed a security guard opening the backdoor with the key. So the security guards did have access to the back.

"I just need to lure one of them over here and then get the jump on them" laughed Benny.

Benny didn't know if the security guards were animal people, either a cat or a dog person. Benny decided to try to sound like both.

"MEOW" said Benny.

Benny attempted to sound like a cat trying to get the attention of one of the security guards.

"That's an odd cat" said one of the security guards.

"I better go check it out" added the second guard.

The second guard headed towards the alleyway where Benny was. Now this particular security guard was a cat person and couldn't resist seeing a cute cat.

"Here kitty, kitty, where are you?" asked the security guard, "I would love to take home a kitty like you!"

Big mistake for the security guard as he turned around, Benny soon grabbed the trash can and tossed it right at the security guard knocking him out - WHAM! Benny soon decided it was time for a change of clothes. He took the security guard's clothes and credentials and soon headed back to where the other security guard was waiting.

"Took you long enough to see if the cat was in the alleyway" said the security guard.

"It was the cutest" laughed Benny.

Benny tried to play the part as he began to observe the other security guard with his badge - CLICK the door allowed the security guard and Benny into the back area of the Nevada Truckers company.

"Now where to start" thought Benny.

The security guard was unaware he allowed an intruder to head inside. Benny immediately headed towards the second floor where the main office of the manager would be. Perhaps he would find some information as he dig further.

"The manager's office, I wonder" thought Benny to himself.

Benny used the security key and surely enough, Benny headed right inside. He didn't know what else he'd find but it'd surely be shocking no doubt.

Episode 3: Suspicious Manager Bao Luc

Benny Dubious managed to make it into the manager's office of the Neveda Trucker Company's office building. It was easy knocking out the security guard, all Benny had to do next was find any incriminating information on the Nevada Truckers and report back to Zafar Mehmet.

"Ha, I'm in, now all that's left is finding the incriminating information" laughed Benny.

Benny continued to search the drawers of the office desk, one by one Benny tried to open them. But then he noticed one of the drawers was locked. He attempted to pull it open with no luck, but then he could hear footsteps coming. The Manager of the Neveda Trucker Company building - Mister Bao Lac was approaching the door. He didn't realize Benny was already inside.

"Gotta hid!" cried Benny.

Benny ducked around into the closet and slammed it shut. Bao soon emerged into his office, he gazed around. Nothing was amiss, but then he noticed the drawers to his office desk were opened.

"That's strange, didn't leave these like this before" said Bao to himself.

Bao then heard some movement in the closet, Benny was doing his best trying to keep calm.

"Is someone there?!" cried Bao.

Benny said not one word to Bao as he continued to hide. He did his best as Benny dove in further purposely getting caught in between the various jackets and coats in the closet. Bao slowly opened the closet door and found nothing. He thought Benny's feet were just shoes left in the closet and shrugged it off. Bao then soon received a phone call - it was from Zafar Mehmet's main rival - Kassim Muhammad.

"Yes boss?" asked Bao on the other end.

"Did you tell the truckers to stop delivering goods to Zafar Mehmet's shipping company?" asked Kassim on the other end.

"Sure did, they didn't like that route anyway" said Bao.

"Good, good" continued Kassim, "I would like for you to prepare for the next stage. You are to send out a report telling every trucking company in the United States NOT to take anything from Zafar's company!"

Clearly Kassim was doing illegal activities such as bribery trying to prevent Zafar from having a fair business. Bao soon began to log onto his computer at his desk. Benny took a glance at the password through a keyhole in the closet. It wasn't a complicated password, since Bao thought no one could break through. As Bao sent the mass email out, Bao was confident this would mean Kassim would give them more money than Zafar.

"Done" said Bao as he sent the email.

Benny wrote the password on his cellphone and also got Bao's login information. As Bao soon got up and left, he soon closed the door. Now all Benny had to do was log back onto the computer and retract the mass email. Benny soon emerged from the closet and soon used Bao's login information. There Benny glanced at Bao's emails and found the mass email he sent to all of the trucking companies.

"Ha, easy said and done" said Benny.

Benny wanted to attempt to sound like Bao so he cracked his knuckles and went to work.

"Dear everyone, I am sorry for the mass email that I sent, I am retracting everything this was all just a misunderstanding" continued Benny.

Benny then hits sent and knew he had to leave immediately. Since Bao also had access to his email on his cellphone, Bao was shocked to see the email before him.

"WHAT IN BLAZES?!" cried Bao.

Bao raced towards his office, but Benny was long gone. The email was already sent! Benny knew he would get paid for helping Zafar dodge a major boycott against his shipping company.

Episode 4: Benny Runs for It!

Benny Dubious sees his chance and makes a run from the manager's office, he could hear footsteps getting closer and closer to him. No doubt it was Manager Bao Lac who wasn't pleased that Benny had sent that email retracting the boycott effort. Benny managed to make it out through the backdoor of the Neveda Trucking Company. A few security guards soon emerged pointing their pistols.

"STOP, INTRUDER!" cried one of the security guards.

BANG, BANG, BANG, the security guards began to try to blast Benny as he did his best to dodge the oncoming bullets. Benny couldn't believe it, he felt he was in the Wild West even though he wasn't. The security guards soon tried to rush towards Benny with their batons in hand.

"STAND STILL!" cried one of the security guards.

The security guards attempted to take various swipes at Benny, but Benny managed to dodge each one. Coming from a former right-hand man of Khalid Jared Muhammad of the White Batch, it was easy for Benny to dodge these moves.

"Ha, you have to do better than that!" laughed Benny.

WHAM, one of the batons managed to strike him but he didn't collapse.

"Okay, you got me that time" said Benny as he regained consciousness.

Benny decided to turn the tables on the security guards and yanked the baton out of one of the security guard's hands. The same guard tried to produce a pistol, but Benny managed to smack it right out of his hand. The other security guard just ended up fleeing. The commotion caught the attention of Manager Bao Lac who noticed Benny was just outside the company building.

"YOU, STOP INTRUDER!" cried Bao.

Bao didn't have any weapons on him, until Bao noticed the pistol on the ground. Benny decided to grab the pistol first before Bao could get his hands on it. Benny soon takes out his own gun and points it at Bao.

"Easy, I just want to escape in one piece, do not try anything at all against me" said Benny.

Benny was doing this as a defensive manner, he didn't want to harm Bao unsure of what he knew about this Kassim Muhammad fellow he was speaking to.

"Why are you trying to boycott my friend Zafar Mehmet?" asked Benny.

"You think you'll get a simple answer out of me?" laughed Bao, "it's rather more complicated than it looks. Zafar and Kassim have been rivals, even before Zafar came to the United States of America."

Benny had no choice but to listen in on why Kassim hated Zafar so much. Kassim was a Lebanese national who wanted to control the trade routes, Zafar's company was ranked number one in the Mediterranean for its shipment of various goods. Bao continued to tell Benny of the story of Kassim's feud with Zafar which originated years before even Benny came to the United States.

"So Kassim doesn't like Zafar, big deal you are messing around my turf" said Benny.

Benny took this information and headed towards his car, but not before Bao was able to call the police. Benny's little intrusion had also triggered a silent alarm that was sent to the police station. Benny could hear sirens were on their way.

"Better get going" thought Benny in his head.

Benny soon drove off, he knew he had to race back to Zafar's mansion where he'd be safe. It took Benny about twenty minutes until he arrived at the mansion. The gates soon opened up and Benny was allowed inside. Zafar could see Benny had caused some commotion though the police were not going to arrest Benny they were arriving to the mansion just to question him.

Episode 5: Red, White and Secure Asset

Benny Dubious arrived back at Zafar Mehmet's mansion safe and sound. Despite the police trying to be on his trail, they arrived at the gated mansion.

"THIS IS THE POLICE, WE WOULD LIKE TO SPEAK WITH THE PROSPECTFUL INTRUDER!" bellowed a police officer through a megaphone.

Realizing this - Zafar allows the police officers in. As they head towards the door after parking their vehicles, they soon realize what sort of individual they were dealing with. Zafar Mehmet was once pardoned by former President Harold Truax. Zafar had infiltrated the Mayoral administration of Madame Mayor Bertha Sole.

"Wait, this address looks familiar" said a police officer.

The police officer soon rang the doorbell and soon instead of a butler answering the door - Zafar answered instead.

"Yes officers, may I assist you?" asked Zafar.

"We noticed an trespassing suspect from the Neveda Truckers Company went inside your residence" said one of the police officers.

"Well, I am afraid I just cannot allow you in, you know President Harold Truax despite being in hiding since his election loss will not be happy if you dare lay a finger on anyone who is a friend of mine" continued Zafar.

The officers froze before moving forward. They debated on what to do next.

"This is the same Zafar Mehmet who was pardoned by a former President" whispered one of the officers as they huddled together.

"I know, but why would the Neveda Truckers have an issue with him?" asked another officer.

The police officers then turned towards Zafar.

"Do you have any issues with the Neveda Truckers to make them suspicious of you?" asked one of the officers.

Zafar knew the Red, White and Secure threat meant that Benny Dubious would be protected for the time being.

"Yes" said Zafar, "they were trying to promote an unauthorized boycott against my shipping company, I suspect that my rival Kassim Muhammad might be behind this mess" said Zafar.

Kassim Muhammad was known to be affiliated with the Blue Eagle Collective more than the Red, White and Secure. It was a way for the Blue Eagle Collective doners to hide their money overseas, not that Zafar himself was doing the same for the Red, White and Secure.

"Well investigating that matter would be out of our jurisdiction" said a police officer, "we would have to forward it to an FBI field office based in Nevada."

Zafar understood and the police officers soon left the mansion without searching for Benny Dubious. Zafar soon headed over to a room where Benny was hiding.

"Benny, they're gone" said Zafar.

Benny sighed with a relief.

"Phew, that was a close one" said Benny, "you saved my neck back there."

"Yes, now you stated you had information on my rival Kassim Muhammad being behind all of this?" asked Zafar.

"Yes, apparently Bao Luc, the manager of the Nevada Truckers building told me everything" continued Benny.

"Yes" said Zafar, "my rival has often done things trying to sabotage my shipping operations. He has even hid among the Blue Eagle Collective to hire Somali pirates to takeover some of the cargo ships."

Zafar was being serious about this with Benny. Benny didn't know what his next moves would be.

"Lay low for a little bit until things have died down, say about at least a day" added Zafar, "you are welcome to anything in my mansion for the time being."

"Thank you for your hospitality" laughed Benny.

Benny soon strolled out of the room, no longer being chased after the police. He soon headed towards the kitchen area of the mansion where he began to make himself a cup of coffee through one of the instant coffee machines. Fresh coffee thought Benny, he would need sometime to rest before going further with Zafar's assignment.

Episode 6: Resting Benny and Kassim Plots

Benny Dubious sighed with a relief as he made a cup of coffee at the kitchen area on the first floor of Zafar Mehmet's mansion. A butler soon arrived asking Benny if he needed assistance with any of the equipment.

"No, I am doing fine thank you" said Benny.

"Master Mehmet insists that we are at your disposal for whatever needs you have" said the butler.

Benny nodded as he took a sip of his coffee.

"Well, I would like to know where I can relax in peace besides the guest room" said Benny.

"Certainly" said the butler.

The butler then shows Benny the entertainment area of the mansion. So many fancy televisions for Benny to choose from. There were even a few video game consoles of the latest brand available.

"Sit, enjoy, have fun" laughed the butler.

"Will do" said Benny.

Benny decided to sit down and watch some television, for Zafar there was never a moments rest. He knew his shipping company was in peril with his rival Kassim Muhammad on the prowl and his right-hand man Bao Luc. Zafar was busy in his study area of the mansion. He gazed out of the window as he watched the last of the police cars disappear from the sight.

"What are you up to Kassim, you were a fool to have hired those Somali pirates to hijack one of my ships" sighed Zafar to himself.

Zafar would have to worry about Kassim's intentions later, for Kassim he was just across from Las Vegas in his own mansion. Kassim Muhammad had been spying on Benny since his arrival. He knew because of Benny's antics with the White Batch as its former right-hand man to Khalid Jared Muhammad would mean quite so much to him. Kassim was busy on a phone call with Bao Luc berating him for his failure in stopping Benny.

"YOU SHOULD HAVE BEEN ARMED!" bellowed Kassim over the phone.

Bao did his best trying to explain to Kassim how he was a pacifist.

"Please, it's not in my nature to be violent" said Bao.

Kassim laughed.

"You should be thinking about training to attack your enemies" continued Kassim.

Kassim had hired Bao Luc through support of the Vietnamese Communist Party's Collective. They were recommended thanks on the part of the Blue Eagle Collective spies. Especially Boss DC who managed to secure Bao's entry into the United States as a naturalized citizen.

"Boss DC did his best to help you get into this country and this is how you repay him?" continued Kassim as he berated Bao.

"I'm sorry, I will try to be more forceful next time" said Bao.

Kassim did his best trying to think on how to get back at Zafar. He couldn't believe Zafar would hire Benny in this fashion.

"Tell me Bao, do you have any relatives who could assist me and my operations?" asked Kassim.

Bao thought of his Americanized niece - Hoa "Mina" Luc. Kassim observed from Bao's own personal social media accounts that "Mina" was a known model on various social media platforms.

"What about your niece?" asked Kassim, "She might be interested in helping us."

"Why bring in my family into this?" asked Bao.

"Listen, if you want to help me cover for your failure for the Blue Eagle Collective you do as I say" said Kassim.

Bao sighed, he knew he would have to find a way to get Mina to assist him. He didn't like being pressured by Kassim but had no choice. His failure in being vulnerable to Benny Dubious did not improve his relationship with his boss.

Episode 7: Getting Mina Involved

Bao Luc after the fateful conversation with Kassim Muhammad on the other end knew what he had to do. As he called his adult niece on the other end - Ms. Hao "Mina" Luc soon picked up on the other end.

"Uncle Bao, what can I do for you?" asked Mina

Mina ran he own salon in downtown Las Vegas, oddly enough she was just a few paces down Benny Dubious' new casino.

"Kassim wants you to try to find any vulnerabilities that this Benny Dubious has" said Bao, "anything that will get him to stop trying to disrupt my boss' operation against his main competitor Zafar Mehmet."

Mina paused and began to look up more information on Benny Dubious. She knew of Benny's name from Los Angeles in some news articles about him operating as a leader within the White Batch a vigilante group that harassed Mayors Bertha Sole and Ted Otenio. She couldn't find that much incriminating information since it was already known information.

"Maybe you can try to work as part of his casino" said Bao, "try to spy on Benny."

Surely enough there were job openings posted for average people to work in Benny's new casino. Benny hadn't paid that much attention over application activities because he was too focused on the tax issue with Nevada's Department of Taxation.

"I will sign up for one post" said Mina.

"Good, my boss will be very pleased" laughed Bao.

Meanwhile, back at Zafar Mehmet's place, Benny Dubious received some notification over a job applicant - Ms. Hoa "Mina" Luc. Benny shrugged off her surname since he knew he needed money. He headed towards Zafar's office where Zafar was doing his best monitoring the restart of the boycott by Kassim against his business.

"I have to go, business duties at my new casino" said Benny.

"Well, take care I think the police will not bother you since I am affiliated with President Harold Truax" said Zafar.

"Yea, it was a good thing that the President did pardon you" continued Benny.

"You are welcome to take any of my cars as your own" added Zafar.

"Thank you" added Benny.

Benny soon headed towards the garage and grabbed one of the keys from a compartment. He then used the key to activate the car. It was a nice, fancy car that Benny had selected. He then got inside and headed back to his casino. He needed to take care of this job application business. Once Benny arrived back, he soon headed inside his empty casino. There were still no patrons at all since he hadn't hired anyone yet. He then headed towards his office where he soon began to send the email to Ms. Mina Luc.

"Sorry about the delay" said Benny as he sent the email to her, "but are you available for a job interview?"

Mina paused as she noticed how fast Benny responded.

"Yes" replied Mina, "I can do tomorrow morning."

"Lovely, see you there" said Benny.

Benny didn't have his usual house yet, so he ended up sleeping inside of his casino. It was a simple way of resting as he pulled out a bed cot. There Benny slept for the rest of the evening, he didn't realize he was falling right into Kassim's scheme. The following morning, Benny got up, he was still dressed in his usual business attire. He headed towards the restroom where he ended up shaving whatever hairs he had on his face.

"Now to have a simple breakfast" said Benny to himself.

Benny headed out of the casino and towards a coffee shop where he picked up his breakfast and coffee. He soon headed back to his casino where he'd be waiting for Ms. Mina to show up.

Episode 8: Disorganized Benny

Ms. Hoa "Mina" Luc soon arrived at the casino precisely around 9 AM, she could see that there was much work to be done with Benny Dubious' own casino. There was a clerk who showed her inside, but the clerk worked for the building manager.

"I am sorry but Mr. Dubious is running a little late" said the clerk.

Mina wondered could this be the same man that tried to infiltrate her uncle's office earlier in the week? Benny soon arrived at the front area of his casino with his coffee and small breakfast meal in hand. She could tell that Benny had a unique background coming from the country of Mali, only to immigrant to the United States. Benny could see this was the woman who responded to the job application.

"I'm Benny Dubious" said Benny as he shook Mina's hand.

Mina could tell that Benny was disorganized, messy and somewhat unkept. She could understand it was his first time running a casino. He always wanted to run a casino, even during his days back in Los Angeles. Benny soon showed Mina inside the main casino entrance. Rather quite empty as Mina glanced around.

"So empty" said Mina, "it needs more employees and customers."

"I'm trying to get to that stage" said Benny.

Benny soon showed Mina the interview area which would be his office. They headed up the elevator to the third floor, and soon Mina sat down in the seat across from Benny's table. Even

Benny's office was quite a mess, paperwork littered all over the place.

"You might need a cleaning person to come in" added Mina.

"Uh, I am still trying to adjust to life in Las Vegas" said Benny.

Benny then sat across from Mina, and the interview began. It was a normal interview, nothing out of the ordinary.

"I run a salon just a few blocks down your casino" said Mina, "I know how to manage and keep things tiddy and neat."

"Good" said Benny, "do you have any references?"

"Well, my references are going to be mostly some of my favorite clients" said Mina.

Mina pulled up a list of clients from her salon, these could be potential customers for his casino.

"I will consider it, you will probably hear from me by the end of the month" said Benny.

The interview went off without a hitch for Mina, Mina could understand how messy Benny was with his casino just starting up. As she headed out, she decided to look into another one of Benny's empty rooms. There was so much mail around, Benny would be too busy looking over her credentials to care. As she did, she noticed a letter from the "Department of Taxation" just lying in plan sight. Benny didn't even have time to put it in a secure location since he was in so much of a rush to help Zafar Mehmet with his problems. She decided to just simply take photos of the letter with her cellphone, simple enough.

"This must be incriminating" thought Mina.

Mina took a few photos of the letter, to make it large enough so that Bao and Kassim could see it. After taking the photos, she ended up heading downstairs to the casino lobby. Benny never had the slightest idea he allowed a spy to operate right under his noise!

"Here is the evidence you have been looking for" said Mina as she sent a text message with the images of the letter to Bao and Kassim.

"Splendid work!" laughed Kassim in a reply text message.

"Yes, nice job, I told you my niece knows her way around Las Vegas" said Bao.

"Great, head back to my mansion and I'll give you your payment for your work" added Kassim.

Kassim was going to embarrass his rival Zafar Mehmet, over a taxation scandal his ally Benny Dubious was in. Aside from that, Kassim was also prepared to tattle on Benny through Neveda's tax regulatory system.

Episode 9: Blackmailing Zafar

Kassim Muhammad was determine to get the drop on his rival Zafar Mehmet. Ms. Hoa "Mina" Luc had just finished her "interview" with Benny Dubious. She had got into her car and headed off towards Kassim's mansion for the payment on her efforts on finding incriminating information on Benny Dubious. Her trip took nearly twenty minutes until she arrived, there she was allowed into the gated mansion where she was greeted by her uncle Bao Luc.

"So glad you made it through that ordeal" said Bao as he let her out of her car.

"It was nothing really, just my specialty in getting the drop on Benny" said Mina.

Mina and Bao soon headed inside, once inside they headed towards Kassim's office. Kassim was very pleased as he got up from his chair. He gave Mina a very warm hug.

"Ah yes, Mina, you did a wonderful job on finding incriminating information on Zafar's ally Benny Dubious!" laughed Kassim.

"What are you going to do with that information sir?" asked Mina.

"Watch and learn" laughed Kassim.

Kassim then began to dial Zafar's own cellphone number. Zafar was just finishing up his breakfast when the cellphone rang. The number belonged to Kassim, wonder what that vile scoundrel wanted from him thought Zafar. Zafar soon picked up his cellphone and answered.

"Yes?" asked Zafar.

"I have a proposition for you Zafar, my old foe" said Kassim, "I will call off the boycott of your shipping company if you do not pay Benny Dubious his taxation fine."

"What are you talking about?" asked Zafar.

Kassim laughed at the other end of the phone.

"Ms. Mina Luc has been very helpful on finding incriminating evidence on Benny Dubious, your wonderful ally of a friend" continued Kassim, "I suggest you tell him to lay off me and my operations or he will have a very bad day with Nevada's taxation regulatory system and more importantly the IRS!"

Zafar was spooked by all of this. How could Benny Dubious allow to interview a spy?! Zafar soon ended the phone call and immediately called up Benny. Benny was doing his best looking through the client list of Mina's that she had given to him earlier when Zafar called him.

"Zafar what's happening my man?" asked Benny.

"Benny you fool, the woman who you interviewed with was working for Kassim!" cried Zafar.

Benny froze in such fright, he was so dazed out from concentrating on Zafar's own assignment he forgot about his own vulnerability!

"Uh, I knew she was too good to be true" sighed Benny.

Benny was rather disappointed, he didn't know what to do on making his next moves.

"Benny, listen to me I hate to side with Kassim but he is right" sighed Zafar.

Zafar knew Benny would be in big trouble if he went any further in helping Zafar out. But he wondered if Benny could go after Kassim himself.

"Listen, Benny Kassim's address is just on the other side of Las Vegas" continued Zafar, "I will provide you with the address if you want a little payback."

Benny thought about it, he thought about the consequences of breaking into the Neveda Truckers Company building just to try to stop the boycott.

"Alright, I will do it, I will have to break into Kassim's residence and teach him a lesson not to mess with Benny Dubious" said Benny.

"Very good and I will reward you with the taxation fee as promise if you do" said Zafar.

Benny thanked Zafar and ended the phone call. He soon received the text message of Kassim Muhammad's address. Benny was determine to get even against the Lebanese national for making a fool out of him!

Episode 10: Kassim's Place

Benny headed towards his car and soon heads towards the address given to him by Zafar Mehmet. Benny couldn't believe how vulnerable he was back there letting Ms. Hoa "Mina" Luc slip by just like that. It was after all, his first year in Las Vegas, Nevada. He didn't know anyone in the Vegas area besides Zafar. Benny's drive in the car took him nearly thirty minutes until he reached Kassim Muhammad's place. Kassim's mansion was much smaller, and he noticed there were guards lurking about.

"Lovely" sighed Benny as he got out of his vehicle.

Benny soon began to creep up towards the bushes, he gazed around. He noticed Kassim's residence was a bit smaller than Zafar's, but he decided to sneak around the back. For some odd reason he noticed there was a fence separating the front and the back. He wondered why, as he peaked through the bushes he noticed at least two large rottweiler dogs roaming around "T-Rex" read one of the collars of the dogs and the other one was "Raptor".

"Figures someone like Kassim would name these two mutts after dinos" laughed Benny.

The rottweilers no doubt were security in the back area of Kassim's residence. Benny needed to be extra careful, he rushed over towards the other area of the back. He could see the dogs were snarling and growling as if they felt his presence.

"Uh, I need to think of a plan" thought Benny.

Benny then noticed a small mom and pop market not far from Kassim's residence. Perhaps they had some sort of treats that he could use in his scheme to get inside. As he headed over to the mom and pop store, the store manager greeted Benny.

"You're new in town" said the clerk.

"I'm curious do you have any sort of dog treats or anything of the sort?" asked Benny.

"Hmm, let me see what I have" said the clerk.

The clerk headed to the back area of the store, and soon came out with a few dog treats.

"There are a few extra dog treats we have usually not for the customers" said the clerk.

Benny handed the clerk at least twenty dollars.

"I will take them" said Benny.

The clerk thanked Benny, and Benny soon headed back to the back area of Kassim's place. The rottweilers were still on patrol and soon paused.

"GRRR" said T-Rex as he glared at Benny's shadow through the bushes.

Benny needed to be extra cautious, he could tell the two rottweilers were hungry. He then began to whistle and show soon emerged from the bushes showing the treats. Raptor and T-Rex soon began to have drool dripping down their mouths happy to see the treats.

"Bet your boss never bothered to give you anything" laughed Benny.

Benny then tossed the treats to the two rottweilers and they began to eat the treats. Benny sighed with some relief, he now had to get inside the back entrance. He began to sneak around the back and noticed an open window. Perfect thought Benny, he soon slipped right through.

"I have to confront this Mina" said Benny, "but also make Kassim pay."

Benny noticed he was in the kitchen area of Kassim's place and soon began to search for some kitchen tools as defense weapons just in case Kassim had a gun on his hand. He slowly began to creep through the residence doing his best not to make any sudden noises. He could hear chatter in the distance one a woman's voice, the others - two males. They had to be Kassim and Bao Luc, he had the element of surprise on his side.

Episode 11: Encounter with Kassim!

Benny Dubious had grabbed a roller from the kitchen, hoping to use it as a self-defense weapon in case if Kassim Muhammad had a gun or a knife on him. He could hear their voices in the distance.

"Benny Dubious is a fool for messing around with my Nevada Trucker Company allies" laughed Kassim, "he doesn't realize the sort of grasp I have on the transportation industry."

"Are you going to tattle on Benny by sending a message to the Nevada Department of Taxation?" asked Mina.

Ms. Hoa "Mina" Luc was smart enough to bring up the letter that she had sent to Kassim and her uncle Bao. Kassim was very pleased, he decided to find the complaint form for the Department of Taxation.

"I do not know if they have arresting powers, but they can forward this information to the IRS and get Benny in trouble that way!" laughed Kassim with joy.

Kassim was about to head onto the website of the Department of Taxation when he heard some footsteps coming his way. He knew it couldn't be one of the security guards since they were outside.

"Someone is inside the house" said Kassim.

"Well, what do you want me to do about it, I'm a pacifist" said Bao.

Kassim then gazed at Mina, he knew he could count on her.

"Mina, I have one more task, please go find out who is intruding around in my residence" said Kassim.

"With pleasure" said Mina.

Mina had suspected it was Benny, Bao didn't know if Mina was being put in harm's way like that.

"Are you insane to put my niece out like that?!" cried Bao.

"Hey, she had more guts to figure out Benny was going to cheat the system" continued Kassim, "I am going to do the system a favor by tattling on him."

Kassim was doing his best trying to search for the complaint submission for the Department of Taxation on his phone. The website was so small, it was hard to see not like a laptop or a desktop computer. For Mina, she was doing her best trying to figure out where Benny was as she was sneaking around the hallway. She could see his figure in the shadows.

"So, you dare break in like a coward?" laughed Mina.

Benny soon emerged with the roller in hand.

"I am going to make you wish you had never crossed paths with me" said Benny.

Benny wasn't the sort of person to harm women at all, unless if he was the victim on the receiving end first. He could sense that Mina was prepared to defend herself.

"You will not get to Kassim" said Mina.

Mina swung her purse at Benny, it was her only tool she could use as a weapon. WHAM, the purse managed to hit Benny right in the face nearly knocking him over. However, Benny managed to pick himself up and charge head on with the roller as if it were a club. Mina ducked, then managed to hit Benny in the groan area. Benny managed to recover and manages to push her out of the way with all of his strength.

"I do not like trying to hurt women" said Benny.

Benny was sentimental over these issues ever since the death of his mother Madame Bokko Dubious at the hands of Taureg rebels in his home country of Mali. Benny knew he had to stop Kassim from any further actions, he ended up bursting through the door and pushing Bao aside. With one swipe of the roller, he knocked Kassim's phone right off his hand!

Episode 12: Unhappy Kassim

Kassim Muhammad couldn't believe that Benny Dubious had knocked the phone out of his hand. He also couldn't believe that the Malian crime boss managed to make it through the two rottweilers in the back.

"So you managed to make it through and pushed away Ms. Mina Luc" laughed Kassim.

"I want you to leave my friend Zafar Mehmet alone" continued Benny, "do not drag my personal issues with your issue with my friend."

Kassim continued to laugh. He was determine to continue the mayhem, however Benny had the upper hand.

"I will not let you continue to impede me from helping Zafar" said Benny.

Benny swung the roller that he held in his hand, Kassim did his best trying to dodge the roller. He then began to hide around Bao Luc.

"What are you doing?!" cried Bao.

"You are going to help me hide from him!" laughed Kassim.

Kassim was no doubt a coward, not willing to fight Benny, and instead use his faithful pacifist helper - Bao as a human shield. Benny didn't seem to care, he kept on swinging the roller, soon Bao found himself dodging the roller as best as he could. Again Benny tried to take a swipe, but both Bao and Kassim ducked.

"You have to do better than that" laughed Kassim.

The entire commotion caught the attention of Ms. Hoa "Mina" Luc who noticed how her uncle Bao was being used by Kassim in such a cowardly manner.

"You dare use my uncle like this?!" cried Mina.

"It's not what it looks like!" cried Kassim.

Mina had enough of Kassim's promises, she swung her purse, Kassim managed to dodge the purse but instead was smacked by the roller - WHAM! The Lebanese national soon falls down, and security guards come running in.

"Well, that's my cue to leave" said Benny.

Benny used the roller to protect himself against the two rottweilers in the back "T-Rex" and "Raptor" were still eating their treats. It provided enough cover for Benny to soon flea the premise. The security guards checked on Kassim, he would be out cold. As Benny got inside his car and started to drive off he knew he had to head towards Zafar's mansion. He could see ambulance sirens in the distance coming to Kassim's residence.

"Better get going" said Benny to himself.

Benny felt relieved that he could get away again. As he drove off, he felt relieved once Kassim's place was becoming a distant memory. The drive back to Zafar took nearly 45 minutes, the gates soon opened from the mansion gate and Benny drove right on in. As Benny parked his car in the garage, he headed out towards the mansion's entrance.

"Master Zafar Mehmet is waiting for you" said the butler.

The butler soon showed Benny inside the mansion, Benny then headed for Zafar's office area.

"I taught Kassim not to mess with you" said Benny.

Zafar smiled, he knew Benny did a bang up job helping him.

"Well, I must say Benny, I guess I owe you that check for 100K dollars" said Zafar.

Zafar soon pulled up his check book and soon wrote him the check. He handed it over to Benny.

"You might be forced to walk this inside the bank to deposit it" said Zafar, "we wouldn't want you to get too much in trouble."

"Nope, it's quite fine doing business with you" said Benny.

"Yes, until next time my friend" laughed Zafar.

As for Kassim Muhammad he was taught a valuable lesson not to mess with the likes of Benny Dubious nor Zafar Mehmet.

Episode 13: Epilogue

Benny Dubious was happy to receive a check of 100K from Zafar Mehmet.

"Take this over to the bank in person so that you are a real person" added Zafar.

Benny nodded and soon left, he then headed towards the garage and took his car and drove towards the bank. Benny soon headed inside the bank, and waited in line like everyone else. Once he managed to make it to the front counter, the teller greeted him.

"What can I do for you?" asked the teller.

Benny gazed at the teller and handed her the check.

"I would like to store this large check in my account" said Benny.

The teller could see that was quite a bit of money - 100K dollars!

"My that's quite some money" said the teller.

"It's for a tax fee I need to pay for the Department of Taxation" said Benny.

"Sure thing, I will take the check and you'll see the money within a few days" added the teller, "you might get a notice over the large sum of money in your account, and a tax form from us."

Benny nodded, after taking the check he soon left the bank and headed back home. Benny didn't have any real place to stay he wanted to see his casino get going first. He could see the various job applications pour in, real ones, not fake like Ms. Hoa "Mina" Luc was. Benny then approved various applicants at random, he was going to be more professional on terms of these interviews. A few days at passed, and Benny soon was scheduling interviews for his casino. These were going to be mostly people who'd man his card areas.

"Now all I have to do is have the interviews and wait" said Benny.

Benny waited, but while he waited he decided to take a glance at the real estate in Las Vegas. It was much more affordable than back in Los Angeles, even though Benny was an apartment person, he wanted something much nicer than what he had back in Los Angeles. All he had was sharing an apartment with his oblivious father - former General Malik Dubious. Benny would have to wait until the revenue would come in. Soon the applicants began to arrive as the week progressed.

"And here they come" said Benny as he waited in the main area.

Many people from all walks of life soon emerged, they were eager to sign up for the various jobs that Benny had posted for his casino. As he began to interview each applicant, they were all eager to have work experience. Many of them were going to fill the bar area of the casino which was rather empty, and a number of them were going to help customers play with the various casino card games. After the last applicant finished his interview, Benny decided to take a stroll down the Vegas Strip.

"Let's see how that salon is doing from Ms. Luc" said Benny to himself.

Benny walked down the strip, as if he were the new crime boss in town. Everyone began to take notice of his white suit and white hat. He soon arrived at the salon of Ms. Hoa "Mina" Luc, she was unhappy with her entire ordeal with Kassim Muhammad on how he treated her uncle Bao Luc.

"Come to rub it in?" asked Mina.

Benny shook his head.

"I want to say there shouldn't be any hard feelings between us" said Benny.

Mina smiled at Benny, she could see that Benny was doing his best to improve his image.

"That Kassim Muhammad is bad news" added Benny, "if anyone who should have a boycott it's him."

"I already put out a post on social media on how he treated my uncle" said Mina, "I am sorry for intruding on you for his behalf."

"Apology accepted" said Benny.

Benny sat down and became one of Mina's customers at her salon, he felt compelled to help her business after what she has been through. That's it for Benny's first adventure in Las Vegas.

Don't miss out!

Visit the website below and you can sign up to receive emails whenever Maxwell Hoffman publishes a new book. There's no charge and no obligation.

https://books2read.com/r/B-A-JVYOC-BJFHF

BOOKS 2 READ

Connecting independent readers to independent writers.

Did you love *Benny Dubious Playbook Scheme: Nevada Shuffle*? Then you should read *Ivan Zhuk: Zhuk's Gambit Book 1 Mental Agony*[1] by Maxwell Hoffman!

Ivan Zhuk finds himself the center of unwanted attention, particularly Yuri Kozlov a Russian mobster and national who has shown distain for Ivan's Ukrainian background. But more importantly, Ivan's presence has the attention of Yuri's rival - Tamrat Hailu, an Ethiopian crime boss seeking to control Chicago's black gangs.

Read more at https://www.instagram.com/vader7800/.

---

1. https://books2read.com/u/mvpRdq

2. https://books2read.com/u/mvpRdq

About the Author

I graduated from California State University with a BA in History. I am fond of historical fiction, science fiction, fantasy, and horror.

Read more at https://www.instagram.com/vader7800/.

About the Publisher

I graduated from California State University of Northridge with a BA in History. I am fond of fantasy, science fiction, historical fiction and horror.

Read more at https://www.instagram.com/vader7800/.